Diane was born in London she was the only child of Pat and Bill Churchman. At the age of three they moved to Essex. Diane was encouraged to read by her parents. Diane loved to read and the house always had books ready at hand.

With love and thanks to Gary, my husband, who, with his never-failing optimism and encouragement, has spurred me on to put this story together.

Diane Westwood

THE MAGICIAN

AUSTIN MACAULEY PUBLISHERS™

LONDON * CAMBRIDGE * NEW YORK * SHARJAH

Copyright © Diane Westwood 2024

The right of Diane Westwood to be identified as author of this work has been asserted by the author in accordance with sections 77 and 78 of the Copyright, Designs and Patents Act 1988.

All rights reserved. No part of this publication may be reproduced, stored in a retrieval system, or transmitted in any form or by any means, electronic, mechanical, photocopying, recording, or otherwise, without the prior permission of the publishers.

Any person who commits any unauthorised act in relation to this publication may be liable to criminal prosecution and civil claims for damages.

This is a work of fiction. Names, characters, businesses, places, events, locales, and incidents are either the products of the author's imagination or used in a fictitious manner. Any resemblance to actual persons, living or dead, or actual events is purely coincidental.

A CIP catalogue record for this title is available from the British Library.

ISBN 9781035842261 (Paperback)
ISBN 9781035842278 (ePub e-book)

www.austinmacauley.com

First Published 2024
Austin Macauley Publishers Ltd®
1 Canada Square
Canary Wharf
London
E14 5AA

Without the knowledge of how to get a book published I approached Austin Macauley and to my utter surprise they contacted me to tell me they liked my book. Thank you all so very much.

Main Character: Mark Sterling:

Early years privately and university educated in Edinburgh, Scotland, known for his shy, bookish manner, excels in all his studies. A tad gawky-looking, wears glasses for close work. Upon attaining his degree/exam results, he is living in student digs with friends. He applied for jobs in finance in Edinburgh.

Eventually, an offer comes in. He is interviewed and offered his first job with money brokers based in Edinburgh: they are **Glen, Roberts & Campbell.** His days are filled with client contact calls for the firm, and during this time, he builds a reputation with clients. The partners of the firm are very impressed with Mark, and he is well-liked by his associates. During a meeting with Blue Chip clients who are based in London and visiting Edinburgh, Mark is asked if he would be interested in a new position based at their firm in London. This firm is stockbrokers called **Rowland Gibbs & Co.** Mark accepted their offer, moved to London, where he would progress to become an analyst with first-line client contact to the Blue Chip firm, trading in the money markets.

Mark is helped by the firm with finding a flat to live in near the City of London. He shares the accommodation with a graduate also working at **Rowland Gibbs.**

Mark's parents live in **Cyprus**: His father is now retired but had served in the British Army for most of his working life, reaching a senior rank. Mark's mother had become ill of late, and they now lead a quiet life in the hills of Mount Troodos. They have few visitors and mostly spend their days enjoying their garden, reading, or listening to music. This was a far cry from the many years when Mark's father and mother lived in many parts of the world and enjoyed an enviable social life.

Once Mark had started his new job in London, he was guided by **Richard Myers**, a senior partner at **Rowland Gibbs & Co**. Richard Myers likes Mark's attitude to work and respects his input at meetings they both attend. They attend seminars and meetings regarding client portfolios. Peter and his deceased wife never had children, and it is possible that Peter found qualities in Mark that, had he had a son, he would have been most proud of him to be like Mark.

Richard Myers was old school in manner and dress. He fitted into the ways of city life perfectly and loved his work. He liked to attend the after-work drinks do's, and he was never short of invitations. Richard was very good company, and people warmed to him. The senior members of the firm trusted his judgement implicitly, and the more junior members felt comfortable with him. And again, he was very well-liked.

Karen Maxwell

Karen was about 5ft 5in tall with shoulder-length, thick, dark hair. She was leggy and full-busted; in fact, she could be considered a head-turner. Always well-groomed with smart business clothes for the office, and a lover of makeup, Karen always arrived at the office looking, some say, rather glamorous. Karen was not an academic like Mark; however, she was ambitious, hard-working, and determined to do well.

Karen had been looking for a new job, and a secretarial agency suggested she attend an interview at Rowland Gibbs. Very excited at the prospect of earning a better salary in an interesting environment, she agreed to attend the interview. Within 24 hrs, she was recruited and had a start date.

Karen was not pushy or overconfident, but her impeccable manners gave her an edge, and she could hold her own with most people. On her first morning at Rowland Gibbs, Karen was escorted around each department by the head of Human Resources. She found it a little daunting, especially the trading area with its lively banter; she felt the eyes undressing her. After she was shown to her desk, which was situated very close to the traders, she could hear the raucous conversations and constant pitch of phones ringing in the background. She felt a little out of her comfort zone but at the same time excited to be, as she considered, in such an elevated environment from her previous job.

Over the following weeks and months, Karen made friends with the other girls and some of the chaps she worked with. She had noticed Mark Sterling looking at her a few times and felt herself blush. He sometimes asked her to arrange business trips for him, and as time went on, they would socialise out of work, mostly in a group. Mark was never seen with a girlfriend, and Karen didn't like to ask about his private life, which he was vague about. They would always gravitate towards each other in the wine bars, have a chat, but often he would leave early. Karen thought he must be going home to someone, and she was always a little disappointed. During the next year or so, Karen found out that Mark was not married or with anyone in particular. As for Karen, she now had a regular boyfriend. Mark would tease her if she left work on time, suggesting she was rushing home to cook for her man. Karen did feel he was a little cutting sometimes, and she would retort that she was seeing a girlfriend, not her boyfriend. In her heart, she knew her feelings for Mark ran deeper than she wanted or would admit.

The next 18 months were turbulent in the City of London, with firms being taken over and people being made redundant. One afternoon, Mark came to her desk and asked if she was busy after work, and if she was free, would she have a drink with him as he had something to tell her. Karen was intrigued but apprehensive; she hoped it was good news. Mark was at the bar as Karen walked in, and he had already ordered their drinks. On sitting down, he became very serious and said he was in a difficult situation and wanted to ask her opinion. He explained he had been approached by an Arab bank wanting to hire him for a senior position, but it would mean being based in Saudi Arabia. Karen's heart sank; she was happy he had been so successful, but the thought of not seeing him each day felt like a body blow to her. She told him he must take the promotion; that's what he had worked and trained for, and this was a fantastic opportunity. He agreed with her and said he was glad she had seen it that way and had wanted her to be the first to know rather than hear it from someone else in the office. Karen could hardly look Mark in the eyes; she knew she wanted to blurt out, "Please don't go." At that moment, a few of their colleagues came over, and they all started to chat. Karen wanted to run away and within 30 mins made her exit, wishing everyone good night. She hailed a black taxi and was struggling to keep the tears from spilling down her cheeks. That night, she cried herself to sleep; she couldn't believe he was going away. At the office the next day, she hoped Mark wouldn't say anything to her; she couldn't trust herself not to cry. Peter Myers came into the trading area, asked for quiet, and made an announcement that Mark was going to be leaving, taking a senior position in the UAE. All of their colleagues congratulated him; he looked a little embarrassed at all the attention. Karen was feeling sick to her stomach; why didn't she tell him how she felt? Even if he had said he didn't feel the same, at least he would know the truth. As is common practice in the City financial area, once you announce you are moving on, then you pack your crate up and off you go to take garden leave before starting at the new place. That evening, we drank at the local watering hole near the office. Karen was dreading it. The evening started with high jinks, lots of laughing, and leg-pulling. The music was blaring out, and they joined in, singing along to the hits of the day. About half-past eight, Karen felt she had to go home; she had drunk more than she usually did just to numb her feelings. She knew she had to go and say farewell to Mark. At that moment, she looked his way, and he was also looking at her in that shy way he had. As she walked over, their eyes locked, and she knew she had to hold back the tears that were trying to fall. With a big smile and in a lighthearted tone, Karen said, "Well, I guess this is it, Mark. I hope you will be very happy, and I wish you every success in the new job." She felt she blurted it all out in a rush but wanted to keep control of her emotions. He looked a little taken aback and then pulled her close, whispering, "You know I always loved you and always will." Karen thought she would faint and quickly turned from him, heading for the door; she could hardly breathe. A black cab was idling near the curb; she asked the driver to take her to the railway station.

Some five years have passed. During that time, Karen breaks it off with her boyfriend and buys a cottage in Kent with some money left to her by her grandparents. She eventually gets made redundant and decides not to travel to London but to work locally. Karen takes a job with a firm of solicitors. She enjoys the work, but in truth, she works to pay her bills. She loves her little cottage and has two Siamese cats for company. She is living a quiet life, but she is content. On one of her rare trips to London to see a girlfriend she used to work with, she is spotted by her boss from back in the day at Rowland Gibb: it's Peter Myers. Peter greets her with a smile and a peck on the cheek. "Karen, how lovely to see you. How are you?" "Yes, I'm doing fine, thanks, Peter. I hope you are well." "Yes, on the whole, but with age come the aches and pains, as they say," and they both laugh. Karen explains she has to catch her train. Peter is meeting a friend, and so they both wish each other well. As Karen goes to move away, Peter offers Karen his business card. He now works from home. Karen looks at the address and tells him, "Do you know, we live quite near each other." "My dear, we must meet up for lunch." "That would be lovely," she replies, "Thank you. I work in **Headborough** four days a week. We could have a pub lunch. I work for Solicitors ***Brookes Fielding Partners.***" "That's a date," Peter says, "I will call you. Karen, take care. So very nice to see you," and they part their ways.

Peter Myers, now a retired director of the London firm Rowland Gibb, had been senior to both Mark Stirling and Karen Maxwell.

Peter Myers was head of trading for Rowland Gibb. He was divorced with no children. Peter is a big man, both in stature and personality, known to be well-liked amongst his peers. Peter was always invited to socialise with his staff and clients alike. He would almost always be found in the midst of a crowd. He is a man of integrity in business and his social life. Peter has a large house in the Kent countryside, surrounded by farmland but within a short drive to the local market town of Headborough and its surrounding villages. He has a housekeeper and gardener who attend his home a couple of days each week. He owns two dogs, is an armchair gardener. He still remains a keen stock market watcher and player with his own portfolio. He gives lectures both at red brick universities and financial firms in the UK and internationally. He drives a Range Rover and dresses impeccably. Peter has a wide circle of friends and contacts around the world.

Over time, Mark Sterling moved jobs, departing the UAE, and is now working in Cairo, Egypt. He is CEO of a large financial firm. Mark is known as **the magician** due to his skill of making huge profits from his investments. His lifestyle could be viewed by some as decadent. He has a large apartment in an expensive area on the Nile Island. He has a housekeeper and attends many parties where the rich and high profile can often be seen. Mark has been said to have indulged in various recreational pursuits, which allegedly may have included dabbling with liaisons with both males and females. He drinks more than he should and finds the pressures of his work weigh heavy on him. Even with all the material gains he has, he never seems to be truly happy. From an outsider's view, his life looks glamorous, but when he is alone, he feels something or someone is missing. Obviously, within the culture he lives, he has tried to be discreet. He is often seen at foreign embassy parties and is invited to attend high-profile client/government-level gatherings. At weekends, his crowd travels out to the wonderful beaches of Egypt. These gatherings get rowdy, and often Mark would wonder why he agreed to attend, as he would have been just as happy reading back at his apartment.

Well, as readers, you have been given a glimpse of the main characters in this short story. So now, I shall begin to tell you of the perhaps sinister yet romantic lives of both Mark Sterling and Karen Maxwell.

After a particularly stressful day at his office, Mark returns home, has a shower, pours a large drink, and listens to music. He always has his laptop at hand and suddenly notices a message from a name he doesn't recognise. The message is direct and suggests it would be in his best interest to be at the Cairo Opera House the next evening. He will have his seat reserved. At the opera, he will be joined by a person who wants to give him something that he will find to be of interest. There is something menacing about the message, and that night, Mark is unable to stop mulling the message over in his mind. The following morning, Mark arrives at his office, still thinking about the request to attend the opera that evening. At the end of the day, Mark goes to the firm's flat above his floor at the office. This is a perk of his job and reflects his status. At the flat, he has fresh clothes especially kept for after-work business functions or private meetings with his superiors.

Once showered and dressed, he pours himself a drink and calls the firm's car service to order a car to be waiting outside the office at 18:45 to take him to the Opera House. In the car, Mark starts to consider what this meeting is going to be about. Cairo is a place of many traditions, secrets, and holds intrigue for those open to such things. On arrival, the car door is opened by the concierge, and Mark, who has frequented the opera many times, is greeted by name and shown to his seat. Almost immediately, a large Egyptian gentleman sits himself next to Mark and greets him with a broad smile, not the smile of the genuine but something dark. "How kind of you to meet me, Mr Stirling. I am here on behalf of *Mr Youssef Sada*. I know you will have heard of him during your time in Cairo." Mark nods. Of course, he knows who Sada is. He is a criminal, very powerful and feared. He is a significant player in money laundering and other black market elements that are believed to be rife in Egypt.

Mark tries to look composed. He can smell the heavy perfume Sada's messenger is wearing; the smell is so overpowering, Mark can't clear his nostrils. "Oh, I see. How kind of Mr Sada to arrange this delightful evening for me." The flunky produces a long manila embossed envelope and passes it to Mark. He chuckles, "It is a pleasure, Mr Stirling. Please do not open this until you reach your apartment. I have to leave you now, *but please do enjoy the opera. Sadly, I have other more urgent business to attend to*. Have a pleasant evening." The flunky is gone almost as quickly as he arrived, but his sickly sweet smell is still hanging in the air. Mark feels intimidated, decides he can't just get up and leave just yet, and sits listening to the music.

The song is famous; it's a version of the **Oum Kalthoum love song called "Enta Omri". Oum Kalthoum was an Egyptian actress and singer famous from the 1920s up until the 1970s.** Revered throughout the Middle East, she is the only female to have a statue in Cairo. The song is legendary. The words to the song are from the heart, and although Mark has heard them on many occasions, it never fails to depress him; it seems to sum up his own life.

Enta Omri

Your eyes returned me to the days that had gone by.
They taught me to regret the past and its wounds.
That which I experienced before my eyes saw you,
What is a wasted life to me?
You are my life whose morning began with your light.
How much of my life before you has passed and gone by.
My darling, how much of my life has gone.
My heart never experienced one bit of joy before you,
And has never tasted in this world anything but the flavour of injury.
I've now just begun to love my life.
I've now begun to fear the time passing of my lifetime.
Every joy that I longed for before you was fantasy.
My heart and mind meet; find it in the light of your eyes.
Oh, life of my heart, oh you who is more precious than my life,
Why didn't I meet your love, my darling, sooner? The sweet nights and the desire and the love for so long,
My heart carried them for you.
Taste love with me,
Taste love with love,

From the feeling of my heart whose desire extended to your feeling.
Give me your eyes; they reflect my eyes in their world. Give me your hands; their touch calms my hands.
Oh, come my darling, come on, forget about that which has passed us.
Oh, you who is more precious than my days,
Oh, you who is sweeter than my dreams,
Take me to your longing, take me,
Pull me away from the universe,
Far, far away, you and I, from the love that awakens our days,
From the desire that sleeps our nights.
I've reconciled time, my days with you,
I've reconciled time with you; I forgot my pains with you, and I forgot with you my woes.
Your eyes called me to the days that have passed. They taught me to regret the past and its wounds.
That which I experienced before my eyes saw you, what is the wasted life to me?

As the lengthy song comes to an end and the 2nd half of the opera awaits, the curtain falls, and the guests clap and vigorously cheer their approval. They start to make their way to the bar; Mark takes the opportunity to leave. As always, taxis are lined up outside the Opera House, and Mark hails the driver at the front of the queue. On arriving back at his apartment, he throws off his jacket, pours a drink, and selects some music. After relaxing and composing himself, he decides to open the manila embossed envelope. He can feel something inside; the envelope contains a CD with a note that reads:

"This is a copy, Mr Stirling. However, for a small favour, the original could be returned to your good self." It was signed by M. Saada. "P.S. Outside of your apartment tomorrow morning at 8 am, a car will await you – you are invited to join me for breakfast at my home where we can discuss this matter in a more comfortable environment. Best regards."

Mark felt nausea creeping over him; his hands were shaking as he put the CD into the CD player. As the CD started, he instantly knew what it was. Mark had indulged in many things since working in the **MENA** regions **(Middle East and North Africa),** always thinking he was careful, but obviously not as careful as he should have been. This CD painted a revolting picture of how he had lived part of his life. He carried deep regret and shame at some of the liaisons he had indulged in. In his heart, he knew he wanted true love but could never seem to find it. The song at the opera took him back to his younger years in London, where he was carefree, life seemed easier, and the laughter seemed genuine. He often thought of Karen Maxwell, his friend, the trading desk PA. How he wished he had made different decisions. He knew she was the person he should have made his life with, but through pride and arrogance, just could never face a possible rejection from her.

That night he slept badly, rose early, and the events of the previous evening came flooding to the front of his thoughts.

As the note said, the car was outside his apartment block; he could see it from his balcony. The driver bade him good morning, and they left his street in silence. As the car moved along his street, which is lined by foreign embassies, he could see the workers going to their respective offices. He knew he was living in a bubble due to his status. Cairo, apart from its historic pyramids and tourist attractions, was a noisy, hot, dirty city full of the poor and hopeless or the very rich and dishonest. He noticed the usual street traders and shopkeepers who no doubt had been at their business for at least 2 hours earlier. Most things in Cairo are done before it becomes too hot. The car drives on, taking a route off of the main road, travelling for about 3 miles before turning into a gated and walled villa, it's gardens like a small park with fountains and lovely seating areas. Mark knew this was all financed by the corrupt businesses Saada was involved in.

Before Mark could put his hand on the car door handle to step out, a servant hurried forward to open the door for him, ushering him into what looked like a marble palace. The place was richly decorated, cool, and tranquil, with many works of art adorning the walls. Mark was asked to be seated, and after 5 minutes, his host appeared with 2 of his flunkies; all three men looked menacing. "Ah, Mr Stirling, good morning. So good to see you. Please, what can I offer you to eat and drink?" Mark replied that coffee would be very nice, and in no time at all, the coffee, with many other delights, appeared. "Well, Mr Stirling, let's get to the reason you have been invited to be my guest. Yes, I expect you are not happy that the CD shows, how shall I put it… yes, the fact is that you are not a man of excellent standing but a weak, indulgent man without self-control. A shame, yes, a great shame, but no matter, we can put things right, I am certain." Saada laughed loudly. Mark felt totally humiliated, but also he felt fear. What was this thug going to want him to do for him?

"Well, I have a little problem, Mr Stirling; however, I am convinced you will be most happy to assist me in putting this problem to bed." Mark clears his throat, "What is your problem, Mr Saada?" Mark asks in what he feels sounds like a trembling voice. "Well, Mr Stirling, my business involves many things, as I am sure you are aware of. I now find that I will need to have someone like your good self to enable me to keep my financial dealings in order—" Saada laughs, "Do you understand, Mr Stirling? I need to be looking very legitimate from every aspect, and this means my cash flows have to be held in safe accounts. Mr Stirling, I want you to be my private banker." Mark's heart is pounding; he knows Saada is under the watchful eyes of the Egyptian Finance Ministry, and his request would make Mark complicit in Saada's illegal and corrupt business dealings. Just being in Saada's home would be a conflict of his interests. "Mr Stirling, you have 4 days to come up with a watertight plan for me. If you do not comply, then the contents of the CD will be exposed to your masters, and your reputation so damaged you will not be welcome in Cairo or anywhere in the MENA region. Do you understand me, Mr Stirling?" "Well, now that it is explained, perhaps you would kindly leave my home," Saada says this with contempt in his voice. A car is outside; go to your office, and I will be in touch.

Mark can feel his legs shaking, and as he walks to the waiting car, he feels his shirt has stuck to his body. The driver says nothing on the journey back to his office, where he drops Mark. Mark goes to the company flat to change clothes and also has a strong drink. He never usually drinks alcohol whilst in the company of his colleagues; this is mostly a Muslim country, drinking alcohol is considered **haram (forbidden)**. Mark goes down to his floor and tries to compose himself—a few colleagues bid him good morning, and everyone carries on with their work. Mark can't concentrate; he has a bad day and can't wait to get back to his apartment. He leaves early; he wants to think about how he can sort this mess out. Arriving home, he showers, tries to calm down enough to think of a way out of this ghastly situation. Around 10 p.m. that night, Mark hears some noise outside his apartment door. He peers into the hallway to see yet another manila envelope. Of course, Saada has more stuff to use against him; this is another CD with contents Mark finds hard to look at. He puts his head in his hands and feels revolted by what he sees. He knows he would be thrown out of his job if this was shown to his superiors and more than likely his visas withdrawn, thus he would never be able to work in finance again anywhere in the Arab world. And elsewhere, he would be a laughing stock; he could even be put in prison.

Music is coming from the apartment next to his; it's a track that Mark used to love back years ago, and the memories of life in London with happy-go-lucky days spent in the City of London with people he could trust. He thought about Peter Miers and wondered if Peter would be open to giving him some advice. Peter was a man of the world, and he had many powerful friends and contacts. Mark decides to contact Peter Miers and sends him an email asking if he would be free to take a telephone call very early the next morning, UK time—Mark apologises for this out-of-the-blue request and for the inconvenience it would cause Peter. An email from Peter comes back in for Mark almost instantly, with the words, **"Of course, I would be delighted to chat."** At 3 a.m. Cairo time, Mark rings Peter; he keeps the details brief, but Peter gets the gist of Mark's situation immediately. Mark explains to Peter that he is being blackmailed by Saada and feels if he doesn't do his bidding, it isn't just his job he will lose. Peter instantly understands and conveys to Mark that if he can stall Saada for 48 hrs, it will give Peter time to speak to friends who will help. It's agreed. Peter will get back to Mark as soon as he can. Mark feels a little easier now he has spoken to Peter. Peter's manner and voice are of a man in total command of all things.

Back In Kent at Peters Myers Home

Very early that morning, Peter calls, arranging to meet an old friend called Kay Richards. Kay is MI6 and informs Peter that Saada is also on their people's radar. He is a violent criminal dealing in money laundering, drugs, prostitution, and, among other things, possible arms trading. "We must meet ASAP to discuss this further. Saada is very dangerous, and your guy needs to get out of this quickly." They agreed to meet in **The Savoy Cocktail Bar in London** the following evening.

Peter has arrived a little early at the Savoy and orders a bottle of champagne and two glasses. As the drinks arrive, Kay appears. Peter kisses Kay on the cheek; they are old friends, and back in the day, Peter and Kay had been close. "Peter, my people are in place to get your man out of Cairo. The plan is he will visit **The British Embassy** and leave via a laundry van in the early hours. The van will take him to the coast, and he will be taken by boat to **Gibraltar**. He will stay at the house of **The Ambassador on the Rock**. They have been informed, so there will be no problem there. Once at **The Gibraltarian Ambassador's House**, he will stay until **An RAF plane** picks him up, bringing him back to Kent, where you will have to find him somewhere to stay that's out of the limelight for a while." They agree on the plan. "Kay, thank you so much. I am very grateful for your help. Mark means an awful lot to me." "Yes, I guessed that was the case. I know you wouldn't have contacted me for anything other than a serious matter." "Peter, it's lovely to see you. Please keep well," Kay bids him farewell, and Peter has the last glass of champagne before heading to the station to get back to Kent and send an email to Mark with details of the plan.

Peter intends to meet Mark when he arrives in Kent, and he can stay at his house for a day or so, but Peter needs to find a safe house. Peter wonders if Karen Maxwell would help. She thought the world of Mark; they were good friends. Would she be willing to be part of this? Should he even involve her? Next morning, Peter rings Karen at the solicitors' office where she works, and they arrange to meet in a local pub for lunch later that day. Peter and Karen are at ease in each other's company, and Peter doesn't wait long before telling Karen what has happened to Mark. Karen is taken aback. She tells Peter any help she can give Mark, she will be glad to. Peter tells Mark to keep Saada in limbo with some dummy A/C details and to get out of Cairo. Peter says his friends have arranged for the British Embassy in Cairo to be briefed, and that they will expect Mark to visit the next afternoon on the pretext of sorting a visa out for a new member of his team. Mark would be covertly taken from the Embassy to Gibraltar some hours later. The last leg of his journey from the Rock would be by RAF aircraft into Kent rather than via Heathrow, etc.

The message to Mark was sent, and the plan was in place, thanks to Kay Richards and her contacts. Mark tells his colleagues he needs to sort out some documents at the British

Embassy and will be back later. He left all his possessions back in his flat, apart from a photo of his parents. His mother and father had been retired for some years and decided to settle in the warm climate of Cyprus. **They live near Paphos in the hills of Cyprus**. Mark's mouth went dry at the thought of his parents knowing of his lifestyle. His mother was very unwell, and he would never want her to know anything of this matter. His father would be utterly ashamed and disappointed in him. On approaching the British Embassy in central Cairo with the Union Jack on the flag pole, Mark feels nostalgic for home. The building is in **Ahmed Ragheb Street, Garden City**, surrounded by grass and gardens. Mark has taken a taxi to the Embassy, leaving his office at around 3 PM. On arrival, he is immediately aware they are expecting him, and he is escorted to an upper floor of the Embassy where he is asked to wait. Very quickly, one of the Embassy staff arrives to explain that the Ambassador has left instructions for Mark to be made ready to depart from Cairo in the early hours of the following morning. For now, Mark is to make himself comfortable in a suite adjacent to the room he is in, and some refreshments will be served very soon. The suite is very comfortable, with TV and all requirements for visiting dignitaries. Mark, by this time, is starting to feel very anxious about the journey to come.

After refreshments have been served, Mark watches some TV to pass the time. At 11pm, he hears a knock at the door. Before he is on his feet, the door is opened, and two officials enter. The two officials explain that at 3am, a laundry van will be at the rear of the Embassy (it is standard practice for the laundry to be picked up and dropped off each week in this manner). Mark will be deposited into one of the large Embassy linen baskets, and it will be loaded into the rear of the van with some other baskets from other embassies that all look the same, apart from the Embassy name on each lid.

A tracksuit is given to Mark, along with a small bag of essentials. "You will be taken to the coast where a boat is docked, waiting for you. From there, you will go to **Gibraltar and stay in the safekeeping of the Gibraltarian Ambassador at the Governor's House on Main Street.** As soon as possible, an RAF aircraft will take you back to Kent where your good friend Peter Myers will be waiting for you. From there on, you are on your own, Mr Stirling. Do you understand these instructions?" Mark clears his throat and thanks them for everything. They depart and leave the following remark hanging in the air – "Well, Mr Stirling, it's too early to thank us. Do that once you are back in Blighty."

At 2:50am, the door opens, and Mark is asked to follow the official down the back staircase where the laundry van is waiting. Once the laundry van doors open, Mark is asked to get into the basket and keep quiet and still until the basket is opened at the dock where the boat is waiting for him.

The journey to the coast seems to take hours. Mark is cramped, hot, and very frightened about what is to come next. Once on the quay, the basket is lifted out, and its lid opened. Mark is ushered very quickly onto the boat and down below out of sight. Mark is not a good sailor and suffers from sea sickness on the journey to the Rock.

A few days later, the boat is being **tied up on the dock at Gibraltar.** Mark is not good on the sea and has had a rough trip, feeling sick. It's a relief to be near to land again. A car is waiting; Mark is ushered away and arrives at the rear of the

Ambassador's residence. Mark is exhausted and apologises to the Ambassador's assistant for his appearance. "We have made ready the small flat upstairs for you, Mr Stirling. Please, let me show you. You can shower and rest. We have some clothes that may be okay for you for your brief stay; they are in the closet." Mark showers and changes. He feels better but still very much on edge. Food and drinks are brought in for him. "Mr Stirling, your stay will be short, but please make yourself comfortable." He conveys his thanks.

Mark covertly looks out of the small upper window from the flat at the top of the **Ambassador's residence. Down below are the guards in place, as always, for the daily changeover, which is done in UK military style and precision. Tourists are taking photographs, and the street is bustling with shoppers, going about the everyday activity of what could be a village in England**. Mark wants to make sure he is out of sight and stands well to the side of the window, behind the heavy drapes.

Before daylight the next morning, Mark is driven to the airport. He is covered by blankets and asked to lie down on the back seat of the vehicle so as not to be noticed. It's very early; the streets are almost empty, at least of tourists. On the tarmac is the RAF aircraft Peter and his friends have arranged for him to be flown back to the UK. Mark looks at the mist hanging over the top of the Rock of Gibraltar (the mist is called the Levant by the locals). The Levant makes the air humid. This mist is said to come from North Africa and is not unusual. Mark just wants to board the aircraft and head home. He is exhausted and feels depressed at his demise. Once onboard, the pilot wastes no time in taking to the air. Mark begins to feel relief and, for the first time since the delivery of

Saada's envelope, has some hope that he may be able to resume his life in freedom.

Back in Kent, Peter arrives in good time to see the RAF VC10 land. He watches Mark come down the steps of the plane. As he got nearer, Peter saw Mark looked thin and tired but deeply tanned and sported a five o'clock beard. He looked rather North African. Peter muses it must be from the years spent in the Arab states. The men embraced. It was evident they had a special bond, a genuine friendship that would never be broken, even though it had been a good few years since they had seen each other.

"Mark, old chap, so good to see you. We are going to my place first so as to get you sorted out and rested. Once you are rested, we can have a jolly good catch-up." On the journey back to Peter's house, Mark thanked Peter for everything he had done for him, saying that he felt he would never be able to repay the debt of kindness. "Old chap, please don't ponder on this blip. Life has many roads for us to travel, and you must concentrate on getting fit and keeping safe and well."

Peter had given both his gardener and housekeeper a few days off so as to keep Mark's arrival from anyone. They would think little of this as Peter often took off for a couple of days and wouldn't require their assistance. Peter would always pay them for the days he laid them off, and they both viewed Peter as a rather special person.

Peter's dogs greeted them, and Peter asked Mark to make himself comfortable whilst he prepared them both coffee and a bacon sandwich – "Oh Peter, the smell of English bacon and good coffee is wonderful. These small pleasures are the things we expats miss the most," Mark confides.

After they have eaten, Peter shows Mark to a bedroom waiting for his arrival. The room has its own en-suite. There are slippers, a towel robe, and shaving cream. Mark can't relax; he is still trying to take it all in. The last week has been like a nightmare for him. Mark reflects on what he has left back in Cairo and is sad to have never been able to say any goodbyes to some very good people, friends he had made over a number of years. Of course, the material things in his apartment could be replaced.

Mark decides to dress; Peter had been kind enough to have left out some clothes that he hoped would be at least of some use for a day or so. Mark selected a sweater and trousers from the closet. It was all rather baggy but of good quality and comfortable for being around the house. Mark could hear Peter talking to his dogs, and as he joined them in the kitchen, Peter explained he was going to take the dogs for their walk.

Peter suggests that whilst he is out, Mark should not answer the phone or the door and advises if he hears movement outside, just lie low. "It will be about an hour." "No problem. Peter, I would like to read one of your books. You seem to have a huge collection." "Of course, old chap, just help yourself. When I get back, let's talk." "Yes, good idea," Mark replies, "I have a lot to tell you, Peter."

The two dogs bark excitedly, and Peter walks down the garden with them and away across the fields that surround the property. It certainly is a lovely spot to live.

Across the fields is a small wood which, apparently, Peter also owns. Peter has done very well for himself over his years in the City, and it shows in the assets he is now enjoying.

Whilst Peter is out, Mark finds a couple of good books, pours himself a coffee, and relaxes. He is unable to concentrate on the books and starts to reflect on how his own life could be very much on the lines of Peter's way of living. He would love a home to be proud of and, like Peter, enjoy the outdoor lifestyle. Cairo was such a far cry from Kent; in Cairo, it was continuous cars hooting and the wails from the minarets calling for the believers to pray. The streets were always congested. The air was full of pollution, and even back at his apartment, he found little peace and quiet, at least not on this scale. You may ask why anyone would want to be in such a place. Easy, his job paid very well. The money enabled him to eat in the best restaurants, travel for holidays to far-off places, and enjoy the historic atmosphere of the Middle East, which, to some, can become addictive.

If you had the money, there was nothing you couldn't get in Cairo. Mark knew he had been indulgent and careless. What a fool he had been.

He had been involved with countless stunning women and also indulged in the dark side of life, which involved parties behind locked doors where cocaine and booze were always available. No shortage of stunning women and also men available to satisfy any appetite. The liaisons he had indulged in, he knew, gave a feeling of risk coupled with fantasy. He knew the people involved were there to take his money or anything they could get from him. Fortunately, he had invested a lot of his money, and it was safe in Swiss banks, so Saada couldn't get to that, at least.

Mark understood if things got out about his past, his career and reputation were going to be so tainted it would be impossible to get employed in the financial world ever again. All the years of hard work and, prior to work, the years at university, all wasted because of his own stupidity and lack of self-control. He felt total shame. His parents were his main concern; he couldn't face them knowing what had been going on.

Mark was almost in a dream-like state, and it seemed as soon as Peter and his dogs had left for their walk, they were back at the house again.

"Any interruptions, old chap?" Peter asks. "No, nothing at all," Mark replies. "Jolly good, that is just what we want. You know, we must look at what your options are, Mark, because Saada is not going to be happy at being fooled, is he?" "You are right, Peter. I have been pondering on just that."

Peter casually comments on their time at Rowland Gibbs. They both recall some of the characters they were working with. Peter then goes on to say, "I am sure you remember back at the old firm, the delightful Karen Maxwell."

"Yes, of course. How could anyone forget Karen? She was a lovely person and very easy on the eyes."

"Well, I bumped into Karen up in town just before I got your email with your bad news. We had agreed to meet up for lunch. The strange thing being, she lives in a village not too far from here, and also works for a firm of solicitors locally. We had lunch the following day, prior to your arrival."

"Oh," Mark says, "is she married now?"

"No, apparently not. The big romance ended some years back, and she decided to leave London. As she got older, she chose a quieter life down here in Kent. She inherited some money from a relative, so it enabled her to move into a rather sweet detached cottage."

Mark states he is very happy Karen is doing well. Peter goes on to tell Mark that Karen has been exceptionally generous, and during their lunch together, on explaining some of the circumstances Mark was in, she had offered to put him up for a week or so until something more permanent could be arranged.

"Oh, Peter, I don't want Karen to be part of this bloody awful situation. I would never forgive myself if anything happened to her. Christ, how much does she know?"

"Only just enough at this stage, don't worry, Mark. It's a good temporary arrangement. She is totally loyal, always discreet, and is happy to help you. Let's be honest, it was pretty obvious you two had an attraction to each other. Most of the office used to wonder why you never got more involved with her. Anyway, Karen is a good cover for you."

"Let me worry about things for now, Mark. I am meeting with Karen tomorrow, and we can fix a time to take you to her place. It's all in hand. She always thought the world of you, and in fact, I had high hopes of you two making something of things. But no matter what will be, will be."

"Peter, I need to be honest with you. Those CDs Saada has contain some explicit and disgusting pictures of how I have conducted my life over the last years. If exposed, they would destroy my career, plus if my parents were made aware of things, it would destroy our relationship completely. My mother is very unwell. I can't stand the thought of how she would feel about me if she were made aware of all this. And Dad would want to disown me. My father is old school. He is a man of honour and self-control over his actions. To see me indulge in such repulsive ways would kill him."

Peter says nothing for what seems like forever, then he tells Mark, "You know, Mark, men have been tempted by many things through the centuries. Yes, this looks very bad. It is an ugly situation, and of course, the damage to your reputation, your career, and the way other people will view you would be difficult for you to come to terms with. But always remember, your parents will never deny you their love. I have been on the brink of bad things years ago which could have destroyed me – oh yes, me, Mr Squeaky Clean. It was an affair with a Russian model; I will leave the rest to your imagination. It ruined my marriage, but I had good friends in high places that were able to limit the damage on my career. And you are in a similar situation, so trust me and think of your future. It won't be the same for a while, but life goes on, and people become used to scandals and bad news. They forget when some other drama comes on their radar."

"You know, I have been thinking ahead, and I feel the best thing is to get you to Germany and then outbound to the States, somewhere off the beaten track where you can have a new identity and chill out for maybe a year or two."

"Oh, Christ, Peter, a year or two sounds like a lifetime."

"Yes, it may, but you will get used to it and may even enjoy a new type of lifestyle. Certainly, it will be different from the Middle East."

"Let me get us both a drink, and I will cook a light meal. We can talk these things through this evening." Peter sorts the dogs out, and Mark can hear him making some food. Sitting there in Peter's home, with its comforts and viewing his lifestyle, Mark feels pangs of envy and admonishes himself again for being such a fool. He too could have all of this, and he has blown it for the dark world of quick sexual gratification, cocaine, and booze – all the things in life that should be viewed with caution, better still, avoided.

The smell of food permeates through into the lounge, and Peter soon returns with an omelette each, ham and salad with some fresh bread. "The coffee is brewing; I will get us a cup in a second," Peter remarks. The food is basic but tastes great. Later that evening, they both enjoy a couple of bottles of wine and recount old times, even laughing at some of the pranks that were pulled back in the day.

In his bedroom, Mark runs the plan Peter has drawn up through his mind. Without any doubt, it is a good idea, and he realises that he will have to lie low for some time. However, Mark is also very uncomfortable at the thought of seeing Karen after so long and under such awful circumstances. But at the same time, he feels his stomach flutter at the thought of seeing her again. Yes, they had been close in many ways, but Mark had messed it all up because of his ego and let her go.

The following morning, the two men discuss the plan more in-depth, and Peter confides to Mark that his friend **Kay Richards** has connections with the Yanks, and that the **FBI** will work with **MI6** on getting Mark to a safe place in the States. Peter also explains to Mark that **Saada** is on the radar of London and the USA for money laundering and drugs but, most significantly, terrorist-funded activity. Both agencies would find it of value to stop Saada permanently.

"Later, after dark, we are going over to Karen's. She is expecting us; everything is arranged." At 10 pm that night, Peter arrives with Mark at Karen's cottage. The cottage sits away from any other property and has its own short but private drive which is gated.

Mark feels agitated; he wonders what Karen will look like; it has been years since they last met. As Peter's car slowly drives up to Karen's cottage, the outside porch lights come on, and he can see Karen is at the front door waiting to greet them.

Peter walks in front, kisses Karen on the cheek, and then says, "Come on, Mark, don't be shy. Karen won't bite you. Karen, it's so lovely to see you," Mark tells her and kisses her lightly on the cheek. He catches her perfume; her hair smells lovely. She looks, yes, of course, older, but not to any huge degree. In fact, she looks even more elegant than in her youth.

"Please come in and sit down, you two, and let me get us all something to drink," she says. "What would you like?" Both say coffee would be lovely. Mark still feels as if this is all a dream. Karen's home is warm and comfortable; it's not grand like Peter's but, like Karen herself, it has an elegance, a warmth; it feels inviting. And he tries to relax.

Karen returns to the lounge with a tray of coffee and homemade cake. They all start to chat about how the years have gone by. Mark starts to apologise to Karen for the inconvenience he is causing. She meets his gaze, smiles, and reassures him, "It's a pleasure, and I am so happy you are well."

Peter decides to make his exit, telling them both he will be in touch very soon. He endorses Mark to lie low and not be seen. After Peter leaves, Karen and Mark both remain formal, but Karen's relaxed manner soon makes it easy to forget the reason he is there. In a short while, they are laughing and chatting as if the lost years meant nothing to them.

"It's late," Karen says, "I will show you your room. I hope it will be OK, Mark, and the bathroom is along the landing." They climb the little staircase, and Karen opens the door to what looks like her guest room; it's feminine, even could be classed as pretty. Mark smiled at her and said, "It's just lovely.

Thank you so very much, Karen. I don't deserve such wonderful friends as you and Peter."

Karen blushes and tells him it's not a problem and to rest, and they can talk some more tomorrow.

At around 8 am, Mark wakes; he is a bit disoriented and looks around the little bedroom with its pretty picture frames and china ornaments. He can smell bacon cooking. He gets up, looks for the bathroom to shower, and goes down into the kitchen. "Morning, Mark, did you get any sleep?" Karen asks. "Yes, I slept the best since leaving Cairo. Would you like toast, coffee? I have cooked some bacon if you want a sandwich or cereal," she offers. "Oh, toast would have been fine, but yes, a bacon sandwich is very tempting."

Karen prepares the bacon sandwich and puts on more coffee. "Mark, I work today until 2 pm. On my way back, I will pick up some shopping but will be back around 3:30. Please help yourself to anything. There is bread, ham, cheese, and salad stuff in the fridge. And the cake tin is full; don't be shy," she smiles.

"Thanks very much, Karen, but I could have fixed breakfast; you should have said you are off to work. Please don't let me make you late." He observes how nice she looks, maybe not as formal as when she worked with him up in London back in the day. Today, she was dressed in a white fitted shirt and black trousers with a hacking jacket. As ever, her make-up was on, hair styled, and he could smell her perfume. "You look very smart," he tells her. She colours and says, "Thank you."

"Well, I have loads of books, CDs, DVDs, etc. Sorry to have to leave you alone, but please have a nice day. And as Peter said, don't answer the phone or door; I am not expecting anyone." "Of course," he replies, "Drive carefully; see you later." Her cats wander in and out of the cat flap; Karen tells him they have been fed. "No worries," Mark tells her. She starts her car and, within minutes, is out of sight. He thinks to himself, "So this is how Karen Maxwell lives her life. How lucky she is; it seems a lovely place to be." He wonders why she is still on her own; she is very attractive, a bit fuller of figure, some signs of grey hair, but has hardly changed facially. She has lovely eyes and a very easy manner. All of her assets, coupled with her nice home, she would, no doubt, have male friends by the dozen.

He pours himself more coffee, puts the TV on, and sits, feeling very at home. How he wishes the next part of his life could include Karen. As she said, at 3:30 pm, her car appeared, coming up the small drive. As she stepped out of the car, he could see she was carrying some shopping. Mark went to the rear door as he was asked not to open the main door at the front of the cottage in case he was, by chance, seen from the road.

They smiled at each other, and he took the bags from her and placed them in the kitchen. "How did your day go?" Mark asks her. "Well, not bad, the usual stuff that local solicitors deal with, nothing of any note. And you, were you very bored?" "No, no, not at all. I watched TV and found a DVD. I hope that was ok." "Of course, it's ok," she chided.

"You have a choice of two for dinner: either roast chicken or lamb chops with veg." "Oh, I love both." "Well," she says, "if I cook the chicken, we can have it cold tomorrow with salad or a sandwich." "Did you make anything to eat whilst I was out?" "I had a large bit of your homemade cake and some coffee. The cake was fab." "Glad you like it. I try not to eat too much cake but bake once a week."

Mark wonders if she cooks for her male friends and starts to ask if she doesn't mind him asking what happened to her boyfriend who Mark thought Karen would marry.

"Oh, you know, it just ran its course, and we went our different ways," she informed him. "Oh, I am sorry." "That was such a long time ago, I don't even give it a second thought," she states.

"And how about you, Mark, did you find a wonderful lady?" "No, no one special, to be honest." He feels himself becoming guarded. He hopes Karen doesn't ask him too much about what happened to cause this situation.

She prepares their evening meal, and after, they sit chatting. Mark navigates around some of the darker parts of his past. Karen would be horrified to know half of his secrets.

"So, what is your next move, Mark?" she asks. "Well, Peter has a few ideas. He is working on it for me. Karen, I won't be staying in the UK. It's not that I don't want to, but it is not possible for me for the time being." "Mark, you don't have to explain anything to me."

"Whatever it is that has caused this situation, I am aware it's dangerous for you to be seen, so that's all I need to know."

"Thank you, Karen. Thank you from the bottom of my heart." She blushes. "It's nothing. We are friends, have been for years, and will continue to be for as long as you want."

"Hey, let's put on some old music from the 80's, see if you can remember them," she says, laughing. They go through her music collection, and as each song is played, they both almost in time say, "Oh, do you remember that bar?" or "What happened to such and such?"

It was a bittersweet evening for both of them. They knew in their hearts that their love was lying dormant, being stifled by circumstance, but would never die and may never be acknowledged by each other.

About 9 pm, the phone rang. Karen answered it, and it was Peter Myers. Peter said he would call tomorrow if it was convenient. Karen said, of course, she was not working and to come for lunch.

Mark realised it was Peter, and Karen informed him Peter was coming the next day. Mark guessed things were moving, and he felt very sad that it would be very soon he would be saying goodbye again to Karen.

For the second night, they enjoyed each other's company, and at times, Karen felt Mark's eyes almost drilling into her head. He knew, as she did, this wasn't going to last much longer. Mark felt he was fighting against himself not to blurt out that he had loved her, did love her, and would always love her. But he knew it was going to be difficult to say their goodbyes. At the end of the evening, Karen told Mark she would tidy the kitchen and that he was welcome to go up without her. They said their goodnights; Mark leaned near to Karen and kissed her cheek. He wanted to hold her tightly but knew it would be the wrong thing to do under the circumstances. With a heavy heart, he headed upstairs.

As arranged, Peter Myers arrived at lunchtime, and the three of them sat, enjoying a glass of wine. Peter tells them both that his contacts have arranged for Mark to fly to **Berlin, stay at an airport hotel**, and fly out to the States within 24 hrs of arriving in Berlin. Karen feels her heart sink and can't look at Mark, and of course, he has similar feelings. Peter passes Mark a slim briefcase and says he has a case with some clothes and a suiter containing a few business shirts, etc. "They should all fit you better than the stuff from my place," he assures Mark. "Great stuff," Mark says, and thanks Peter. He says he can pay for the clothes as he has A/Cs in Switzerland.

"No, old chap, I am afraid that from the day you leave Blighty, you can't be who you are for some time. You must start your new life and be someone else." Mark's heart sinks, and he just nods his head, eventually saying, "What am I thinking? Of course, I can't use any cash from those A/Cs." "But Peter, how can I repay you?" Peter looks them both in the eyes and says, "You know, when you get to my time of life and have the chance to do someone a small kindness, it gives such pleasure. Of course, your situation certainly does not give me pleasure, Mark, but I know you will bounce back, and your life will become even happier than before. Forget about money, just keep safe."

Peter explains that money will be available in Berlin at the hotel reception. A deposit box has his new name on it. After this conversation, Karen becomes even more concerned for Mark's safety. She knows the measures that Peter has taken to sort things out for Mark have gone far beyond the normal 'friend helps friend'.

The evening continues in a more light-hearted mood; Karen opens another bottle of wine. Peter declines the wine, as it means he would be over the limit if he has another glass, so tells them it's time for him to go home. Before Peter leaves, he tells Mark he will phone to give him a time that he will be picked up. "Old chap, I won't see you again for a long time, no doubt, but I will always hold you dear to me. Don't let me down." They both feel emotional, and Peter doesn't turn around but gets into his car and drives away. Mark feels he has feet of stone and suddenly is aware of Karen asking him if he is okay. "Sorry, Karen, I got lost in my thoughts." "Yes, I can see, and it is very natural that you feel this way. You are out of your comfort zone. Who wouldn't feel concerned?"

"Thanks, Karen. You have always been, and are, a wonderful friend." She smiles, touches his arm. "Come on, let's sit and finish off the wine." Before they sit down, Mark takes Karen's hand; she can feel him trembling as he pulls her close to him. "Karen, I have fucked my life up in so many ways, and I have so many regrets. Why didn't you make me see the truth years ago? You know we should have been together." "Mark, it's not that I didn't feel love for you, but my pride wouldn't allow me to show you just how deep my feelings ran. I felt you should go away and have the career you had worked so hard for, and also, it would not have been right for me to pursue you. It should have come from you. I always hoped you would get in touch. But the years fell away, and my hopes faded." "Oh Christ, what a stupid waste. We could have had a wonderful life with each other. These years have been wasted just because of our pride, and now our pride has paid us back, hasn't it?"

That night, they slept in Karen's bed and held each other close, comforting each other. Karen is aware of how terrified Mark must be feeling. Mark would never do anything to hurt Karen, and with his past unknown to her, he is torn apart that he can't show her how much he loves her in a more physical way.

The next morning, Karen is presented with coffee, toast, and orange juice in bed. "Wow, you are an old smoothie," she jokes with him. He blushes, gets back into bed, and they eat their breakfast. Mark asks Karen if she is seeing anyone, and she says no, there hasn't been anyone for a long time. She is hesitant to ask about Cairo, but he tells her that he has been with a number of women but never truly wanted anything permanent and never loved them either.

Later, downstairs, the phone rings; it's Peter. He delivers the news Mark and Karen were dreading. "Tonight, old chap, be ready to leave at 10 pm. You will be taken to the aircraft and fly out to Berlin by charter flight. There will be cash, your air tickets, a new passport, and visa. It's all been taken care of by my good friends. You will be shadowed by friends from the UK and USA until you reach your destination. The destination will be revealed later for your safety."

"Peter, I will repay you, I promise." "No matter, old chap, just don't break Karen's heart, will you?" "She has broken mine, I am afraid," Mark states. "Yes, I thought that may be the case. Not all is lost, believe me. Goodbye, and good luck, Mark."

Mark tells Karen the latest news. She tries to hide her feelings, but it's obvious how they both feel. That night, as Peter had arranged, Mark was ready to leave Karen. As the car for him neared her front door, Mark pulled her close, telling her he would like to hold onto her for the rest of his life. She had tears in her eyes and could just about tell him she too wanted just that. Very quickly, he was gone. Again, he had left her, and again, she was heartbroken—perhaps even more this time because of what had now been said by both of them.

She turned off the lights and went to her bedroom. As she undressed, she noticed two folded sheets of paper on her dressing table. As she read the contents, she broke down in floods of tears. Mark had left her the following love poem:

Enta Omri

Your Eyes Returned Me to the Days That Had Gone By.
They Taught Me to Regret the Past and Its Wounds.
That Which I Experienced Before My Eyes Saw You.
What Was the Wasted Life to Me?
You Are My Life Whose Morning Began with Your Light.
How Much of My Life Before You Has Passed and Gone By.
My Darling, How Much of My Life Has Gone.
My Heart Never Experienced One Bit of Joy Before You.
And Has Never Tasted in This World Anything but the Flavour of Injury.
I've Just Begun to Love My Life.
I've Now Begun to Fear the Time Passing of My Lifetime.
Every Joy That I Longed for Before You Was Fantasy.
My Heart and Mind Meet, Find It in the Light of Your Eyes.
Oh, Life of My Heart, Oh You Who Are More Precious Than My Life.
Why Didn't I Meet Your Love, My Darling, Sooner? The Sweet Nights and the Desire and the Love for So Long,
My Heart Carried Them for You.
Taste Love with Me,
Taste Love with Love,

From the Feeling of My Heart Whose Desire Extended to Your Feeling.
Give Me Your Eyes, They Reflect My Eyes in Their World,
Give Me Your Hands, Their Touch Calms My Hands.
Oh, Come My Darling, Come On, Forget About That Which Has Passed Us.
Oh, You Who Are More Precious Than My Days,
Oh, You Who Are Sweeter Than My Dreams,
Take Me to Your Longing, Take Me,
Pull Me Away from the Universe,
Far, Far Away, You and I, From the Love That Awakens Our Days.

Karen, shaking with emotion, prays Mark will keep safe and one day return to her.

The next day she has to work, she has puffy eyes and feels very emotional. Her boss notices she is not her usual bright self, "Karen, you don't look well, I think you should go home. Have a couple of days off, you look very tired." She protests that she is fine but **Mr. Price, her boss, and one of the senior partners** at her place of work, is a kind man and in the end, she agrees to just go home today and be back in the morning.

On arriving home, she makes coffee; she can't eat, she feels so sad, she can't stop thinking of Mark. The next couple of days pass and she has, as promised, to go back to work. Life has to start getting back to normal for her. In fact, all that has taken place feels rather dreamlike.

Peter Myers has made a number of arrangements and needs to contact Karen to once again ask for her help.

They arrange to meet in the same pub as before, which is halfway between Karen's place and Peter's house. They hug each other as father and daughter would. "How are you, Karen? It must be so difficult for you." "It is difficult, Peter, but I wouldn't have had it any other way. You understand us both, and it's probably been clear to you for years how it was for us back at the old firm." Peter empathises with her but tries to get her to see the upside of things and that, as he told Mark, not all is lost.

"Karen, I need another favour from you. How do you feel about a few days in Cyprus?"

"Cyprus?" she repeats, "Why **Cyprus**, Peter?" "Mark's parents have retired out there, and his father needs to be put in the picture. Mark's mother is very unwell, and if she thought Mark was in this type of trouble, it could make things so much worse. Oh, of course, I remember him saying his parents lived abroad." "Why me, Peter? Would you not like a few days out in the sun?" "I can't, Karen, I have some other urgent business to attend to. Everything will be paid for, Karen, so no worries on that score. I want you to take on the guise of **someone looking to buy a villa in the hills of Paphos.** Do you think you could do that? Whilst you are looking at a few properties, I want you to go and visit Mark's father and mother, and explain to them why they have not heard from him and won't be hearing from him for some time." "Oh, Peter, this is very, very serious for Mark, isn't it?" "Karen, I will spell it out. It is right that you should know. You see, Mark could be murdered by an Arab drugs baron and his thugs if he is found. They were blackmailing him, wanting him to launder their ill-gotten gains." Karen gasps. This was beyond anything she could have imagined. She had been utterly naïve.

"I will have to take leave from work, but that shouldn't be a problem. My boss is kind and has said I look a little tired, so he won't suspect anything is odd about me taking a few days off. Ok, it will be arranged, Karen. I will make sure every move you make keeps you out of danger as much as possible, but you must have your wits about you. As regards how much you tell Mark's father, it's up to your discretion, but he should know at least the bones of this debacle."

As they part, Karen is apprehensive at what looks to be a dangerous task, but she will do it for Mark, no second thoughts.

The air tickets plus hotel reservation arrive; she books some annual leave. Over the next few days, she arranges for her cats to be fed whilst she is away by a neighbour and sorts her clothes out for the trip. Onboard her flight, she starts to mentally go over how she will present herself to Mark's parents, "Looking for a villa is no problem, in fact, it sounds like a great idea." Karen takes her flight, albeit she is nervous about what is ahead of her.

As they come into land, Karen checks her documents/confirmation for her hotel reservation. Once through the checking area, she wheels her small case outside of the airport and hails a taxi. She asks the driver to take her to her hotel. The hotel staff can't be more helpful, and her room is on the 4th floor, overlooking some stunning views. She unpacks, showers, and decides to have a walk around and buy coffee and a sandwich. Karen registers her interest with 2 estate agents in the town; the staff are very keen to show her the most recent properties on their books. She agrees to view 2 the next day. After dinner that evening, Karen decides to have an early night and think about the visit she must pay to Mark's parents. She has the cover of looking at a few villas on the market and intends to view them prior to visiting **The Stirling's home**. Had she been intending to make a purchase, she would have found it easy to find a suitable place. After the viewings and back at her hotel, she asks the receptionist to arrange for a taxi to take her to Mark's parents' home.

She decides, although it's very hot, to wear a suit and look business-like; this would cause no attention as she arrived looking smart and viewed the villas looking like a business person.

The driver was given the address, and the car pulled away into the **Aphrodite Hills of Paphos.** The area is so very beautiful, and she can understand why Mark's parents decided to make Cyprus their retirement home.

As they arrive outside of the Stirling's villa, Karen asks the driver not to wait but just to give her time to make sure the homeowners are in. She mentions that she will call for him in under an hour for her return journey to the hotel. Smoothing her clothes and adjusting her hair, she swings her legs out of the car. She pays the driver and thanks him.

She feels nervous; this isn't going to be easy, and she is not looking forward to the possible reception she may receive. She walks down the drive past wonderful plants, trees, and climbing vines; it's a beautiful villa. She rings the bell, and almost instantly, a tall, slim elderly man who looks so very much like Mark opens the front door.

"Hello," she says, "Are you Mark Stirling's father?" "Yes, I most certainly am," she can hear in his voice. He is a proud father. He smiles and bids her hello and asks, "What can I do for you?"

Karen, in a soft voice, explains she has some news for him about his son. Mr Stirling looks horror-struck, "My goodness, he is ok, isn't he?" "Yes, yes, Mr Stirling, he is, but I need to explain some things to you." He asks her to come inside and shows her into the lounge. She hears a woman's voice from upstairs calling him and asking who has arrived. He asks to be excused and is gone for just a minute, "I am sorry, but my wife is very unwell; she is bed bound." "I am very sorry to hear that, Mr Stirling." "Please, sit down," he gestures to a comfy-looking armchair. He asks if she would like any refreshment, maybe an ice-cold drink or tea/coffee. Karen smiles and thanks him but says it's fine; she has just had some lunch.

"Well, Miss...??? Sorry, you didn't give your name. How rude of me. I confess to be concerned about Mark; your arrival worries me." "Please, don't worry. I understand my just turning up must be alarming for you. My name is Karen Maxwell. A long time ago, Mark and I worked together at **Rowland Gibbs in London.**" "Goodness, that was a while ago, Miss Maxwell," she asks him to call her Karen. "So, Karen, what is Mark's news? What is so important that he has to ask you to visit us?" "Mr Stirling, I am here to tell you Mark has found himself in trouble back in Cairo. In fact, he was being blackmailed by a known criminal." She sees him go pale, "For goodness' sake, how would he get himself into that sort of circle?" "I can only tell you what I know, and that Mark is not in Cairo right now. He initially spent a few days in the UK; I understand he is now somewhere in the USA."

Mr Stirling, Mark will have to lie low for some time. He has been given another identity and sadly cannot visit you for fear of his life. His father starts to look tired, and his face has become tense on hearing her news. "I don't know what to say, Karen, and will find it even more difficult to tell his mother. Have you travelled from London to see us?" "Well, just outside London. I live in Kent. Mark stayed with me for a couple of days, and a mutual colleague with a lot of clout has made all the necessary arrangements for Mark."

Mark's father says how grateful he is that she has let him know and, of course, it's dire news, but at least his son is safe for the time being. "Please convey our sincere thanks to your friends on our behalf," he asks. "I will, of course, and for you, my dear, you have been so very kind. Thank you very much." Karen tells him it's not a problem, that Mark is so very well-liked and respected, he has good friends.

She explains she is leaving Cyprus the next morning and asks if she could call the taxi firm to get her back to her hotel. Mark's father asks Karen if she will keep him informed with any news of Mark. She assures him she will do everything possible to help Mark and also him and his wife. He looks at her and says, "You know, Mark must have made a very good impression on you for you to go to such lengths for him."

"Yes, you could put it like that," she smiles. She hears the taxi stop outside of the villa and bids Mark's father goodbye. She conveys her kind wishes to his wife and wishes her health to improve. Mark's father takes her hand and puts his other hand over hers, and again thanks her. He is such a gentleman, Karen thinks, and how much like Mark. She walks down the drive to the waiting taxi.

Mark's father stands at the door until the car has gone. Back at the hotel, she showers, has a sandwich, and settles on the balcony in the warm late afternoon air. Next day at the airport, she buys a magazine and waits at the boarding gate to get back home.

Peter is at the airport waiting for her in arrivals, "Karen, are you okay? How did it go?"

"Well, it all went to plan, Peter. Mr Stirling Snr was so very nice." "Yes, he is a nice chap; I only met him once. Mark was out to dinner with both of his parents, and I was at another table."

Karen asks if there is any word from Mark, and Peter tells her he is waiting to hear and, as soon as any news comes in, he will let her know. "Well, let's get you home, Karen."

Once back at Karen's cottage, she asks Peter if he would like a drink. He says he could do with a gin if she has one. "Would you like it with ice and tonic?" "That'd be great," he says. "You also must need a stiff drink after all that you have done, Karen." "I do," and they both sit sipping their drinks.

"How did it all go with Mark's father, Karen?" "He was so sweet. It was obviously not what any parent wanted to hear, but, as explained to me, he was very much old school, like yourself, and has an excellent coping manner. Mark's mother is so unwell; she is bed bound. It must be very difficult for them." "Yes, I bet it's bloody awful," Peter agrees.

"Peter, you do think Mark will be okay in the States, don't you?" she questions. "Well," he replies, "it seemed like the only option, especially knowing his enemies would pursue him if they could."

"What will he do for work?" "Don't you worry; that is all sorted out, and I can only say that it will be difficult for him at first, but the role he is going to be undertaking, he will enjoy once he settles in. I have been told he will be a senior lecturer in physics and maths. He had stars from university in all his subjects, so it should be a breeze for him." "Goodness, that is so much more of a sober job than all he has already done, isn't it?" "Yes, but it is a must, as they say."

"Karen, I will be off now. You need to get on after the trip, and I have to attend to things back at the house. I'll ring you in a few days, but don't hesitate to call me if you need anything." "Thanks, Peter." "No, I am the one to give you the thanks."

She walks him to the front door, watches him get into his car, and drives down the drive onto the road.

Karen runs a bath, pours another gin and tonic, which she takes upstairs with her. In her room, she finds Mark's letter, and again the tears well up. She admonishes herself and tries to pull herself together. She has to carry on just as before he briefly came back into her life. She feels a deep sense of loss.

Mark left Germany and arrived in the States. He is checking out at customs and thinks about who will be waiting to meet him. No sooner has he cleared all the checking points when he hears his name, that is his new name, **which is Oliver Graham**. "Mr Graham, I hope you had a good journey, sir." "Yes," Mark says, "Thank you." The guy introduces himself, "My name is **Steve O'Connor**; I have the pleasure of showing you around town and to your apartment, which is near to the campus." Mark had been briefed in Berlin as to what he was going to be doing in the USA. "Oh, thanks so much. I appreciate that. My vehicle is just over on the lot." Mark feels the heat envelope him as the doors of the airport automatically open for them, and they stride outside. "I don't think you will need a jacket, Mr Graham," Sir O'Connor laughs. "No, I was just thinking the same thing myself," Mark replies.

Arriving at his apartment, Mark tries to imagine his new life, his new job, and how he wishes he could magically the next year or so away and try to get to see Karen and Richard again.

"Mr Graham, I think you will find everything you need. The refrigerator has been filled, and should you need anything, your vehicle is in the lot outside. These are the keys." Mark thanks O'Connor and closes the apartment door. He looks out of the window, watching O'Connor disappear down the road.

On the table are some files marked for his attention. Mark decides to shower, see what food is in the kitchen, and sit to read the instructions he assumes are in the files.

The new job is in the university; it's just a 10-minute drive away. The day before he is due to start teaching, Mark drives down to have a look at the place. The graduates all seem quite well off with their own cars; the area itself is upper-middle-class. It seems like a very nice place.

Six Months Pass

Over the last few days, Mark has pondered on the Saada situation. He is ruthless, and Mark hopes that by being in the USA, he will be out of his reach.

Mark is making the best of his new job and new life. The staff and most of the graduates are decent people, and the work is hardly a challenge for him.

Mark is often asked to dinner with his new colleagues or to attend the baseball, which he enjoys. He looks well, has gained a little weight, and is sleeping much easier than for a long time.

One evening, after university, Mark is preparing work for his students for the next few days. In the background, his TV is on, and out of the blue, he hears the name **Mohamed Saada** – Mark freezes, listening intently to **CNN reporting** that in a drugs raid, Saada, just outside of Cairo, Saada and his cohorts have been killed or arrested. For Mark, this brings him up short with thoughts of how this will affect his own situation; he wonders if it will soon be safe to leave the USA and go back to the UK.

The next morning, Mark is woken early by the doorbell to his apartment ringing. Standing in the doorway is **Steve O'Connor** – "Good morning, **Mr Graham,** special delivery from friends." Mark asks O'Connor to join him in a coffee; O'Connor declines but thanks Mark for the offer. "I am off out of town for a while, but please read the contents of the papers inside this file. I am pretty sure you will be very happy with its contents. Mr Graham, I wish you well. I can imagine the last few months have taken a huge toll on you. So, sir, please take care in the future."

Mark bids O'Connor farewell and thanks him for everything. Sitting at his kitchen counter, Mark looks at the contents of the large envelope O'Connor delivered; it contained money and air tickets to London. Covering the contents is a note saying 'Godspeed.' Mark feels very emotional but pulls himself together and gets ready for another day at the university. This will be a day that he has to speak to the principal and give him notice that he will be going home to the UK.

On Mark's final day, his new friends hold a little farewell drinks party, and he is given a scroll and a plaque with kind words about his time with them. It is, in a way, a sad day, but of course, Mark is also overjoyed that he will be going home.

The day he has yearned for arrives, and all his travel arrangements run smoothly; the flight back has no delays. Waiting at Heathrow, he sees Peter close to the check-out area. They hug, and Mark tells Peter how glad he is that he is home.

On the journey back to Peter's house, Peter tells Mark that there is going to be a welcome gathering on his arrival – "Yes, it's your parents and, of course, Karen."

To date, Mark and Karen are living in Karen's cottage in Kent. Mark teaches Maths at a local school. They lead a quiet life but, of course, see Peter Miers quite often for dinner or drinks. On balance, out of a very dark place, much has been gained because, at long last, Mark Stirling is the happiest he has ever been with the woman he has always loved. Peter Miers has the son he would have liked but also a daughter too.

Mark's parents are back in Cyprus; his mother is a little better. They do come and stay in the UK for Christmas etc. Mark is very wealthy; all of his money is in Swiss bank accounts, and Peter has made both Mark and Karen beneficiaries to his assets and his house. But the money means nothing in comparison to the peace of mind and leading a stress-free life being with the people who mean the most to you.

The writer of this short story hopes you have enjoyed reading this part factual and part fictional tale and hopes to meet with you again in the future.